The

Comet Cat

A.C. Winfield

The Comet Cat

Text © 2014 A.C.Winfield
Cover & illustrations © A.C. Winfield

All rights reserved.

This is a work of fiction. All names, characters,
and events are a creation of the author's imagination.
Any resemblance to persons living or dead is purely
coincidental.

No part of this book may be reproduced, stored in
a retrieval system, or transmitted by any means,
electronic, mechanical, photocopying, recording,
or otherwise without written permission of the
copyright holder, except as provided by UK
copyright law.

ISBN-13: 978-1495355172
ISBN-10: 1495355179

For Dest x

Acknowledgements

Once again I must thank my Mum who is simply
the best!

Also to all my friends, fellow crafters from
St. Andrew's Street Craft Centre, my work
colleagues, and anyone who has shown me support
over the past year and spurred me on to keep
writing my stories.

A special thanks goes out to Vickie Johnstone for
your excellent editing skills and patience. Also to
Susan and Jane, thank you for your guidance and
continuing support.

A big thank you to my sister overseas, who has
helped me a huge amount in making this book come
together, and also to her daughter who rescued a little
cat and inspired me to write this particular adventure.

And, once again, thank to you for reading and
following Ebony's Legacy.

So THANK YOU everyone!
Ax

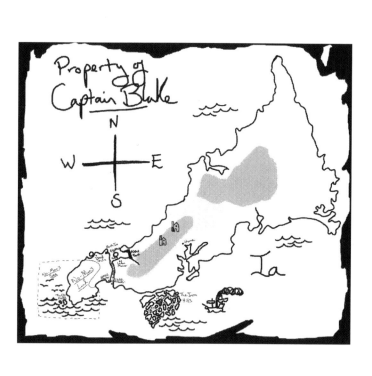

The Comet Cat

E bony was not like any other child in the
mysterious land of Ia. The girl was brought
there during a time of need, and even though neither
she nor the people of Ia knew it, she was the world's
only hope in the time of the Great War. An innocent
soul caught up in the clashes between the Humans and
the Eternals, Ebony's light shone the brightest of them
all, for she was the daughter of the land, sea and stars.

Ebony loved her bedroom. She could step out on
to her balcony and look out over the beautiful gardens
far below. The grounds of her home, Ladon Manor,
were vast and the girl's favourite part was tiny
compared to the rest. It comprised of a stretch of
grass, very long, wide and rectangular in shape.

Around its red-brick borders lavender grew very tall, full of fragrance, making the bees buzz merrily. Even from her balcony door, Ebony could smell the wonderful scent, wafting in on the breeze.

To the left and right of her bedroom ivy grew, clawing its way up the red walls of the manor where she lived with her grandfather. When the days started overtaking the nights the swifts came and built their nests along the stone pillars and ledges. How their muddy homes stuck to the walls always amazed Ebony. The little girl would befriend the baby swifts. When they spread their tiny wings and flew across the sky for the first time, she noticed how they would only travel a short distance.

One night after taking her bath, Ebony thought about the little birds while sitting on her grandfather's lap. As he brushed her dark, frizzy hair, she asked him, "Why don't the baby swifts fly away, soar up into the sky high above and never touch the ground ever again?"

Her question made him chortle. "Ah well, you see, my dear Ebony, until their tiny muscles grow big and strong, their parents won't let them fly very far from home. Watch them closely and you'll see that during the day the babies may play close to their nest, but come nightfall they will be sent to bed by their mum and dad. Talking of which, I think it's time for your bedtime, young lady."

"Aw!" Ebony moaned, but she snuggled under her woollen blankets, ready to be tucked in by her grandfather. She loved the night as much as the day for she was a child of both worlds.

***

For many nights since returning on the back of Mother Star Bear after her last adventure, Ebony would wake with a start from a recurring dream. This particular one was about her parents. In the dream she would find herself running alongside her mother in the form of another Star Bear, just like Ursa Major and Ursa Minor on the painted ceiling of the library; their fur matching, like their eyes, in every way.

Stars shone brightly up above, guiding their way along a well-trodden path. Mother and daughter would only stop once they reached the cliff's edge, unable to go any further.

There, far below, waving from his deck stood Ebony's father, Captain Blake of the pirate steamship *Fire Crow*.

The little girl's dream seemed so real and it was only when she imagined the sun rising once more, when night gave way to day, that she knew she had to say goodbye to them again. She treasured her memories of her parents and missed them dearly, for it was such a long time since she had last seen the two of them.

Ebony's grandfather knew how much she missed them. "You'll see them again, love," he told her as she sat on his lap after telling him a mighty fine tale of how Captain Blake had slain a giant lobster that was trying to sink his ship. The creature was then cooked by the chef and fed to the crew.

"Just keep your eyes peeled for your mother's star," the old man reminded her.

"I have been, Grandfather, honest," she piped up.

"And you still haven't seen her star?"

The girl's lip wobbled.

"Hey now," he soothed, jolting Ebony up and down as though she was on horseback. Just as he knew that tapping her on the nose would make his granddaughter smile, so this was also a way to lessen her woes. "Just because you can't see her doesn't mean she's not thinking about you," he said, kissing Ebony's head softly. "Your mother and father will always feel your presence here," he added, patting the place over his heart.

The old man then placed a finger underneath his sulking granddaughter's chin, tilting her head upwards so she was no longer looking at the beeswaxed floor. He looked deeply into her brown, golden-streaked eyes and for a moment a fond memory came back to him of his own daughter, Stella Night, now a mighty Star Bear – Stella Maris, the Northern Star and Navigator of the Seas.

Ebony frowned, misunderstanding her grandfather's emotional reaction as the trail of thoughts crossed his mind. To her, he seemed as sad as she was, but inside he was actually smiling. He was content to have the memories of his daughter to hold on to, and, of course, her own daughter to look after, just as he had promised all those years ago.

Just as Ebony was about to ask him what the matter was, he surprised her by tweaking her nose gently. "Got your nose!" he cried out, making his Great Dane, Dominic, leap up and bark with excitement, thinking his master had a ball. The old man held his hand up high, his thumb between his fingers, as his granddaughter stood on his bony legs, trying to reach the pretend nose he just stolen from her.

"Hey, give it back, Grandfather," she said, chuckling. And just like that their sadness was forgotten, for they still had each other.

***

Sometimes Ebony's grandfather would have to go away on business, leaving Strict Bea in charge. As a reward he would bring home a nice gift for the girl – a doll, a wind-up toy or maybe even a pretty dress – but ever since she had gone away with her parents, her sense of adventure had increased a great deal. Now, dresses and dolls did not have the same appeal. Instead, the old man had to bring home maps and reading instruments every time he went away.

After a while the girl had a fine collection of objects that she thought would help her to become an explorer or even a sea captain, just like her father, when she was older, for Ebony Night knew she was really a Star Pirate. After all, her father was the pirate captain of the steamship *Fire Crow* and her mother was a mighty Star Bear, with fur the colour of the blackest black, bluest blue and all shades of purple. When she returned to the sky, she became the Northern Star, Stella Maris, Navigator of the Sea. Together, her parents were the 'Protectors of Ia'.

After a time, Ebony gained a compass, a magnifying glass, a set of binoculars, a calliper and a strange device that her grandfather called a sextant. She did not fully understand how to use this particular instrument, but she loved to look through it and pretend she was back on board the *Fire Crow*, measuring the distance between the rising moon and where the starry night sky met the land below. The sextant glistened in the sunshine as it stood majestically on its stand; its copper and brass surface gleaming as brightly as any unearthed treasure. To Ebony, this was one of her most prized processions.

The girl longed to travel beyond Ladon Manor's grounds and explore every corner of Ia, but her grandfather wanted her to stay inside the boundary walls. She did not think this rule fair, but crossed her heart and promised him anyway. On some of the sunniest days, however, when it was too hot to be anywhere else apart from beside the shady lake's waters, Ebony would wave up to the old man as he sat in his study, from which he waved back through his window.

Her grandfather would watch her with his steel-grey eyes as she made her way down the steep, earthen slopes until it was no longer possible for him to see her dark, frizzy hair bobbing as she skipped away merrily, wondering what today would bring. Perhaps she would pretend to be sailing the high seas or exploring the dark forests or maybe, just maybe, she might bump into an Eternal! As Ebony skipped along the winding, sloping path, she imagined all of the questions she would ask the nightmarish being if she did happen to stumble upon one during her exploring.

Ebony took with her some paper coated in wax to waterproof the boats she planned to set sail upon the surface of the lake. However, once out of sight of her grandfather's window, she changed her mind and slipped into the forest beyond. There she followed a little stream that wound its way down the shady valley. Perched on top of the highest part of the ancient stone wall, she sat in silence, listening to the birds chirp their songs to one another.

At the base of the valley was a clearing. A little distance away was marshland where the trees' roots could not take hold, framing a line of fields full of munching cows, before you reached a little village that hugged the river's edge. To the little girl, no rules were being broken. This was the boundary wall, so it wouldn't hurt to sit and watch from here…

Chapter 1
The Wish

C ORRR!

The noise made me jump. Lucky I was quick or the fall from the wall would have really hurt.

COORRRR!

I turned. Up on a nearby branch was perched a large, inky black rook. I told him off – "Look what you made me do!"

COORRRR!

The rook looked at me, blinking his beady, silver-rimmed eyes once, twice, three times, before spreading his feathery wings and taking off. He soared up through the treetops, his velvety wings blocking out the bright sunlight for a few seconds. It was only then that something else caught my eye – movement down below. Was I imagining it? The rook had vanished, along with his shadow. But something moved again, so I stood up on the wall for a better look.

I quivered with excitement. Alongside the boggy stream was a group of children sneaking towards Ladon Manor's boundary wall! I jumped up and then ducked down again. I had never seen any kids from the village this close before. In the past I had seen some of them in front of our gates, pushing and daring one another to go inside, but every time I went to see what they were up to, Sunny shooed them away before I could talk to them. This time I was determined to meet them, but then I thought of my promise to Grandfather. I couldn't break my oath. I loved him far too much to do that. Sitting down, I thought long and hard, and after a little while I had an idea.

Crouching, I sneaked along the old, crumbing boundary wall, careful not to be seen by any of the children. Then I ran down the valley until I reached the lowest part where the stone wall had collapsed. I knew this area well. This was where I liked to watch the deer jump in and out of the manor's grounds. Before I ran out of wall to hide behind, I took a quick peek at the group and realised they were making their way towards me! I heard them getting closer and closer, and then, suddenly, they stopped.

"Go on!" egged on one of the children.

I peeked over the wall. A girl with straight, blonde hair had spoken. She was the tallest of the bunch.

"Why don't you go first?" dared the lad she was talking to, as he pointed up towards my home. He had straight, blonde hair too.

"Because, brother, this was your idea, unless you are too chicken?" replied the girl, who started making clucking noises, flapping her arms and scratching the ground with her feet.

The other children laughed. There were five of them in total: one girl and four boys.

"Hi!" I greeted them, jumping up on to the low wall. While I was not allowed over this boundary, no one had ever said anything about talking to someone on the other side.

All of the youngsters gasped. I laughed quietly to myself as I watched the four boys cower behind the girl. "If you want to come see Ladon Manor, I don't mind showing you around," I offered.

The tall, blonde girl stepped closer to me. Even with me standing on the wall, she was the same height. I noticed she had the same beady eyes as the rook. "Who are you?" she asked sharply, looking me up and down.

The situation reminded me of the first time I was recruited on board the *Fire Crow*. My father, too, had inspected me before declaring that I was a member of his crew. Perhaps this girl wanted me to join her group of friends too! "I'm Ebony Night," I answered. "I live here at Ladon Manor."

The girl just stared at me, her eyebrows rising all the way up until they were lost in her fringe. She looked at her brother and friends, who all seemed just as surprised, but then, slowly and simultaneously, they grinned at one another. As she turned to me, she was smiling. Thinking they were just shy to begin with, I smiled back encouragingly.

"You live with the old man up there?" she asked, pointing up at the manor house, which was peeking out of the trees.

I nodded. "Yes, he's my grandfather."

All of the kids laughed.

Glancing at the boys and then back at the tall girl, I asked, "What?"

Acting as one, the group stepped forward. The movement was so sudden and unexpected that it was my turn to be surprised. I backed away, forgetting that I was up on the wall. Losing my footing, I fell on to my bottom. Luckily, the mushy, leafy ground softened my landing.

I picked myself up, quick as a flash the children clambered over the wall and circled me. Feeling like the piggy in the middle, I frowned, unable to understand their actions. Did they want to play? I was about to ask when the blonde boy said, "So you're the one!"

My fists tightened into little balls. I didn't know what he meant by that, but I did not like the way he said it. Something inside me cried out for me to run!

"I am the one what?" I asked, standing my ground. I was a Star Pirate, a member of my father's crew and the daughter of a Star Bear. Who had heard of such a person running away?

The tall girl laughed. "You're the one who they say was abandoned on Lord Ladon's doorstep."

My stomach dropped and my mouth fell open.

"Your father is dead, your mother is dead, and you've only got that old man to keep you company!" she blurted out with a viciousness that I had never heard anyone use before.

I found myself shaking and replied, "That's not true." My eyes started to sting and I could hear ringing in my ears. "My mother didn't abandon me. She…she…" I couldn't get my words out. My face was wet from the streams of salty tears now running down my hot cheeks.

"Oh yeah?" jeered one of the boys, who strolled up to me, kicking some twigs out of his way. He was broad and had a closely shaven head, making him look older than the other lads. "How come you're here with no parents then?" Plucking up one of my plaits from my shoulder, he held it between his fingers, wrinkling up his nose as though it smelt of something bad.

"Hey!" I yelled, surprising the boy a little as I knocked his arm away. "Stop that."

Now it was the blonde girl's turn again. "I bet your mum and dad saw you and ran away," she teased, doing the same thing to my hair. All of the boys laughed.

"Did not," I spluttered, shaking my head in a bid to pull my plait free from the tall girl's grip, but she held on tightly. "Ouch!" I cried out, and all the children just pointed at me and laughed even more.

"Oh, I'm sorry," the girl said.

I didn't trust her; her lip wobbled too much.

"Did that hurt?" she asked me, but this time she did sound like she was trying to be kind.

"Yeah," I told her, taking my plait back, uncertain what to make of her sudden change of heart.

"Oh, boo hoo!" she yelled loudly, making my ears hurt.

I watched as all of the kids rubbed their eyes, making faces and pretending to cry like babies. "Whaa and boo hoo!" the blonde repeated, continuing to touch her eyes. "Who are you going to run to, the old man?"

The group stepped even closer to me and I could hear drumming in my ears. I couldn't see any way out of the circle. "My father is a pirate captain. If… if you don't be careful, he and his pirate crew will…" I trailed off as the children roared with laughter around me. I tried again, but stumbled on my words. All bravery had flown away with the inky black rook.

"Will what?" asked the boy who was the smallest, even more so than me, but being surrounded on all sides, I still found him frightening.

"My mother…"

The faces of the crowd lit up, and I watched in terror as their grins grew wider and wider.

"We're listening," the blonde girl sung out, cupping hold of her ear.

I shook my head, not wanting to tell them anything else. They were mean; meaner than anyone I had ever met. How could anyone be this horrible? At that moment all five of them reached out and tried to tug my hair.

"Stop that!" I yelled, turning with all my might. The children lost their grip on my plaits, but it hurt a lot. I rubbed my head where the strands had been pulled.

"What was that about your mother?" the girl asked again. Her voice had changed once more, sounding kind, but I knew she was pretending.

I looked at each of the five children in turn. The lads were shoving one another, whispering behind their hands, but the girl stood as still as a statue, her hands held together in front of her gingham dress, fluttering her eyelashes at me. Maybe she was going to tell her friends to be nicer, so why was I getting that same feeling to run? I shook my head.

The girl stepped closer. "What was that about your mother?" she asked again, her blue eyes sparkling slightly in the dappled light.

I backed away, bumping into the shaven-headed lad, who shoved me back into the middle of their circle. "She's a Star Bear," I told them, but before I could say any more the children all bellowed with laugher – so hard that they held their sides as they bent over, clinging onto one another to stay upright.

"Stupid girl!" spluttered the blonde-haired girl between giggles.

My face felt like it was burning.

"You were abandoned and left here… alone…"

Before I could hear any more, I shoved the shaven boy out of my way and ran as fast as I could. Mud splattered against my back and head, its dark, sticky mess coating my once silky hair.

"Run back to your old man!" one boy cried out.

"Stop telling lies!" the others yelled after me, trying to keep up as they threw more mud at me.

Even when my sides hurt, I didn't let myself slow down. I ran to the nearest unlocked door that led inside Ladon Manor to safety. I heard the girl scream,

"Ebony Night is such a loser," but her voice was distant. The group must have stopped on the path at the outer edge of the woodland. I leant against the closed wooden door, struggling to get my breath back. The distance did not stop the children's hurtful words from floating through the gap between the door and the flagstone floor.

"No," the blonde boy said, trying to catch his breath and laughing hard as he shouted, "She's a loner – Ebony Night, the loner!" I heard the others join in, singing the words over and over again: "Ebony night is a loser, Ebony Night is a loner."

I tried not to listen, but their voices did not want to stop. The last thing I heard was their laughter fading away as they trudged off back home. All seemed quiet until… "Ebony Night! What have you been doing?"

I jumped, but then breathed a sigh of relief as it was only Bea who called my name now. She was astonished to find me all covered in mud. The hair she had so carefully plaited in the morning were now untied in a ragged mess. My eyes stung, and my face was warm and sticky from my salty tears.

"What on Ia?" Bea exclaimed as she inspected me. "What happened?"

I ran forward and hugged her waist tightly as she guided me, squelching, all the way upstairs. By the time I finished telling Bea my story about the mean village children, my bathwater had turned a muddy brown.

"Let's get you out of this tub," she said, wrapping a warm, thick woollen towel around my shoulders as she lifted me out. "Kick," she added and I did, splashing off the excess water.

I was still shaking as Bea dried me, but at least the strange feeling to run had left me. Taking another towel from the rail, she started rubbing my hair dry. "Well, Ebony, unfortunately that's some people for you. You tell them the truth and even if it's true, people won't want to believe you. You tell them a lie and they'll believe you just like that." Bea stopped rubbing my hair dry for a moment and clicked her fingers. "You can never win."

When she took the towel off my head, I could feel my uncontrollable black hair tingle as it stuck up all over the place. My face still felt warm, but my tears had dissolved long ago in the muddy bathwater.

Bea looked at me for a few seconds. "You want to know my advice?" she asked me and I nodded. "Don't tell anyone the truth."

I frowned, making my nose wrinkle up.

Bea felt my hair for any wet strands that had escaped her relentless drying. Finding one, she continued, "I hate to say it, little miss, but there are some cruel people out there, even ones around the same age as yourself." She stopped in mid-action, looking deeply into my golden-streaked brown eyes. "Don't tell your grandfather about this incident, alright? It'll only make him upset. I'll deal with the ruined clothes."

I nodded, unable to take my eyes off Bea. My mouth hung open as I watched her wrap my soggy, muddy clothes inside the now wet towels, hiding them from view. Never before had I thought of Strict Bea as Nice Bea, but right now…

Frowning, she then told me, "You mustn't tell anyone else the truth. Your grandfather told you never to go outside Ladon's boundary walls, but I don't think that's enough. Nobody outside the manor must know who your mother or father is, okay?"

I frowned back. "But why can't I tell them?" I asked, unsure why Bea would say such a thing. If anyone else had a pirate captain and a Star Bear for parents, surely they wouldn't keep it a secret?

"It's for the best, Ebony," she replied, taking the first piece of clean clothing off the rail. It was a purple dress with sunflowers embroidered on the pocket, which she held out for me to put on.

"But why?" I asked, determined not to get dressed until she told me.

"Ebony," Bea moaned, rubbing her face that was still a vivid pink from the bath's hot vapours. She stopped and gazed at me. Her next question was one I would never ever forget: "Ebony, why do you think your grandfather keeps you here?"

My furrow deepened, crinkling my face all the way from my scalp to the top of my nose. "Keeps me here?" I repeated quietly, not understanding what she meant by that; somehow it sounded strange. Why wouldn't grandfather keep me here? This was our home after all.

Bea waggled the cotton dress in front of me as a reminder that I was meant to be getting dressed before my grandfather found out about the mean children. I slipped it over my head. As I did so, I heard her words become slightly muffled as she added, "Look, just trust me. Don't tell anyone who you are. Just pretend you are a regular kid from the village or something. Someone... well, normal."

27

As my head and arms popped through the openings in the dress, Bea placed one of her hands on my head. She tilted her body in a funny way to one side until her head was again level with mine, looking at me upside down. I laughed.

Bea could be funny when she really tried, but that was only sometimes. I could even count the number of occasions on my fingers without using any of my toes: the time I fell and cut my knee on the gravel drive; when I bounced too high on my bed, slipping off the end and banging my head; the time I plunged out of the tree; and when I fell off the boundary wall, though Bea never found out which wall. Although she could be strict, she was never a bully like those mean children.

"Now off you go to dinner. Your grandfather will be wondering where you've got to," Bea said, nudging me gently out of the bathroom door with her foot.

I laughed. Despite being Strict Bea, she was funny at times, if she really tried.

***

It was the night on which I had told my grandfather the story of the giant lobster that ended up on the dinner plates of the crew of the *Fire Crow*. I was tucked up in bed and he kissed me on the forehead. After making sure the curtains were wide open, so I could keep an eye out for my mother's star, he said, "Goodnight, my little Star Pirate."

"Goodnight, Grandfather," I answered, making him smile. His eyes crinkled in the corners and he left the room.

I waited until I could no longer hear his footsteps before running towards the doors to my balcony. Throwing them wide open, I stepped out and there she was! My mother, Stella Maris, the Northern Star, shining so brightly that the heavens glowed a hue of midnight blue.

I could not help but gasp as I spun around in a circle, my arms open wide, staring up at the night sky way up high. Stopping, I lowered my eyes and leaned over my balcony wall. Below, I saw the grass glitter as the dew sparkled like tiny midnight-blue crystals littering the ground. Then I looked back up at her, my mother's star, and smiled widely. I should have known that she would understand. After all, ruling the stars must be lonely sometimes too.

As I continued to gaze up at her, a shooting star lit up the sky a little brighter than before. As it zoomed across, I spotted two tails on it, instead of one. I waved up at it, laughing, as it seemed to twinkle back at me.

"Make a wish, Ebony," my mother's voice carried on the cool breeze.

I stopped waving and clung tightly to the railing in front of me. Scrunching up my eyes, I sent a silent prayer to the twinkling, moving star. "I wish I could have a friend," I thought over and over again.

Opening my eyes, I found that both my mother's and the shooting star had vanished from sight. My lips wobbled. I was alone once again, having missed my chance to wish upon a shooting star. I had lost the chance to tell it how much I needed a friend to play with; one who wouldn't be mean to me and would make me laugh when I felt sad; someone I could tell about my father, Captain Blake of the pirate steamship *Fire Crow*, and about my mother, a Star Bear, Stella Maris, the brightest star in Ia's night sky;

someone to whom I could tell all my adventures and the stories from my book, *Ebony's Legacy.*

Turning away, I ran back through the balcony doors, slamming them shut, and I clambered into my bed. The tears started as soon as I threw the covers over my head. All I wanted in the whole of Ia was a friend.

"Please make my wish come true," I whimpered in the dark.

Chapter 2

A Bump in the Night

I miss my friend, Misty. It was thanks to her that I finally met my parents. At first I had been frightened of her, but in the dark everything seems scary. Every bump, squeak, creek and knock. Misty was the only source of light when I travelled through the dark mines and from her I learnt to not be afraid of the dark. She also taught me not to fear those who seem different. You never know, they might turn out to be a good friend.

Misty was certainly my best friend, but she had to leave me. I am very sad about that, but I am happy for her as she found her family and other friends again.

***

It was three nights after I wished upon the shooting star that I spotted my mother's Northern Star in the heavens once again. I lay on my side as I watched her watching me. She shone brightly and I imagined her lighting the way for a lost sailor across the sea. Then, suddenly, I heard a strange noise.

I sat up and frowned, which surely made my nose crinkle in a funny way. Holding my breath, I strained my ears, but as hard as I tried, I couldn't hear the odd noise again. After a little while I lay back down on my bed, watching my mother watching me as she guided some lost sailor across the sea... but there it was again! Once more, I sat up and frowned, held my breath and strained my ears, but this time I did hear something.

Bump! "Mew!"

There was movement by my bedroom door. Something was in my room! I was scared, I was shaking and I gulped, but then I remembered the time I met Misty in the dark. "Be brave. Whatever it is, it's probably more scared of you," I assured myself. Wasn't that what grandfather always told me about spiders? Ah, I hoped it wasn't a giant one!

"Hello?" I called out.

Bump! "Meeewww!"

I leapt out of bed. Whatever it was did not sound like a spider, but more like... I spied movement by my desk. There was a loud clang and my bin fell over.

"Meeeeewwwww!" the thing squealed.

"Hello?" I said again.

I realised the something was behind the place where my tin bin had been. As it rolled away, the something in my room watched me with its bright green, diamond-shaped eyes. They reminded me of my friend, Misty, for she used to have strange glowing eyes and I no longer felt afraid. "Hello?" I said, kneeling down. "Don't be afraid. My name is Ebony Night."

"Daughter of the Northern Star and Navigator of the seas?" asked the creature in the dark with the bright green, diamond-shaped eyes.

I nodded. "That's right and my father is Captain Blake of the steamship *Fire Crow*."

"Ruler of the waves?"

I nodded. I was not sure if the creature could see me in the dark, but I noticed its glowing eyes blink slowly. "Do you believe me?" I asked excitedly. Not wanting to frighten the poor thing, I crossed my legs ever so slowly and waited on the rug for it to answer.

After a little while the green eyes bobbed. "I do not know them personally," was the reply.

I could now see the dark form of the creature coming towards me slowly. "But I have heard of their stories – beings of both myth and legend meeting here on Ia," it continued. "And you must be their offspring – daughter of the land, sea and stars?"

The dark form stepped out from underneath my writing desk and sat in front of me on the rug. I took an intake of breath. In front of me sat the cutest black cat I had ever seen! In the bright starlight cast down from my mother, its belly looked speckled, patterned like a scattering of glowing stars. Its head, which was framed by long, white whiskers, seemed slightly too large for its body. The cat's ears sat on top, pricked up into perfect points. They twitched from side to side, listening for the smallest squeak or snuffle.

"What's your name?" I asked.

"Hale," he replied, licking his paw, which he used to wash his face.

"Why are you here?"

"I fell," said the cat with the speckled belly and a head framed by wispy whiskers.

I scratched my head, just like grandfather did when he was puzzled. "But what happened exactly?"

Hale stopped washing and stared up at me with his glowing green eyes. He blinked once slowly before answering, "I fell from the night sky."

My mouth dropped open in amazement. "What is it like up there?" I asked, excitedly.

"It was fun," Hale replied. "I chased the constellations of the Hare, the Dove and the Crow across the heavens. I am the fastest of all my brothers and sisters."

"You don't eat the Hare, the Dove or the Crow when you catch them, do you?" I enquired out of concern for those who dwelt up there. Maybe he would chase Mother some day, but then I shook my head. No, that was silly as she was much bigger than this night cat sat on my bedroom rug.

The creature with the speckled belly and a head framed by wispy whiskers chuckled. "No, they are my friends. We merely play tag."

"Oh," I replied, very relieved. I smiled at Hale and he grinned back, his teeth flashing in my mother's starlight that shone brightly through the balcony doors.

"But, why aren't you playing with them tonight?" I asked. "Why are you in my room banging into my things? Why aren't you with your friends up in the night sky, playing tag? Why did you fall?"

Hale's smile vanished. "Because of this," he replied, showing me his tail.

There, beside it, was a small stump. My eyes grew wide.

"I was a twin-tailed Comet Cat," he said sadly, "but now I have only one."

Chapter 3

Hale's Tale

I knew Hale was not your usual kind of cat that liked to sit in the sun all day. He preferred to chase the Hare, the Dove and the Crow across the night sky. The four friends played every night as Hale was the fastest of all Comet Cats. The Hare would run while the Dove and Crow flew. No one, it seemed, could catch them except for Hale – he could outrun them all! All night long he would chase until he eventually caught all three.

Hale's fur was as black as the night and the speckles on his belly shone as brightly as the stars themselves, but what made him different from his siblings and other Comet Cats were his twin tails. These enabled him to balance perfectly between the tightropes of the constellations hanging in the night sky.

At first Hale felt lonely, just like me. He was considered different from all the other cats, but when the constellations of the Hare, the Dove and the Crow saw how fast he could run, they soon let him join in with their night-time games. He found himself no longer alone and since that night the four of them were best friends.

One day, while Hale was playing with his three mates, he heard a voice call out, "My, my, Comet Cat, how Glos-s-y your fur is!"

The cat was so flattered that he stopped in his tracks to see who spoke. It turned out to be the constellation Snake that was complementing him.

"Thank you," he replied.

"My, my, Comet Cat, how wonderful are the s-s-starlight speckles upon your chest," Snake continued.

Hale felt even more flattered. "Thank you."

"My, my, Comet Cat, how beautiful your tails-s-s are!"

"And thank you again." Hale, being very fond of his tails, flicked them back and forth to show them off better. The two night creatures admired them for a little while in silence. Hale realised that the Hare, the Crow and the Dove were getting away, but he also knew he could catch up with them very easily.

The Snake shifted his giant belly, his scales rattling as he sighed sadly, "I wis-s-sh I had a tail such as your-s-s-s."

Hale looked up at Snake's head and down along his long body as it curved in the night sky. It disappeared over the horizon and stretched far into the south.

"But you do," the cat told him. "You have a magnificent tail. I have seen it myself. Your scales glitter so brightly in the moon's light."

"Thank you," Snake replied, "but my tail is in the s-s-south. I am too long for the human-s-s-s to see. How will the people on Ia ever know what I really am if they cannot s-s-see my tail? If only there was-s-s a way of having a tail here in the northern sky, so they can s-s-see that I am the constellation S-S-Snake?"

The little Comet Cat thought long and hard. Glancing at his twin tails, he had an idea, but he was afraid to speak it aloud. Hale liked his tails, but Snake's sadness reminded him of how lonely and sad he had been before the Hare, the Dove and the Crow became his friends.

Thanks to the two tails helping his balance, Hale had been able to run fast with the three of them along the tightropes of the constellations, joining in with their games. Perhaps if he let Snake borrow one of his tails, even for a short while, the people down on Ia would be able to see it in the northern sky. Snake's constellation would then be recognised and he would never feel lonely again.

Snake was very grateful to Hale for letting him borrow his tail. For the rest of the night the cat played chase with the Hare, the Dove and the Crow, but with only one tail he could no longer keep up with them. Hale often lost his balance along the tightropes strung across the night sky and toppled over when turning to the left or right. One tail might be fine for his brothers and sisters, but Hale was born with two and he felt lost without them both.

The next night, Hale approached Snake and asked, "Have the people of Ia noticed your new tail?"

"Thank you, Comet Cat, for your generos-s-sity," he replied. "The humans-s-s down on Ia have been looking through their telescopes-s-s and jotting me down on their charts-s-s. They only need one more night and these shall be complete."

And so, Hale let Snake borrow his tail for one more night. Meanwhile, the Comet Cat played with the Hare, the Dove and the Crow, but, like the previous night, he could not keep up. The poor cat kept losing his balance and falling off the tightropes.

The following night, Hale approached Snake again and asked, "Have all the people of Ia noticed your new tail now and recognised your constellation?"

Again, Snake thanked the cat for letting him borrow his tail, but again he made an excuse. "These humans-s-s have been looking up into their telescopes-s-s and are plotting my movements-s-s closely. I need one more night, so they can get their charts-s-s just right."

43

Hale's one tail twitched with annoyance, but then he remembered how sad Snake had been before the people of Ia began to notice him. Perhaps one more night will not do any harm, he thought.

Later, Hale played with his friends again, but the fact that he could no longer keep up made him very upset indeed.

On the third night the Comet Cat went back to the Snake and pleaded with him, "Please give me back my tail," because he wished to chase his three friends across the night sky.

Snake answered, "The humans have been looking up in their telescopes-s-s and are plotting my constellation in great detail. I think they will even give me a new name very s-s-soon. I need one more night, little Comet Cat. Tomorrow I will be forever recognised as the mightiest of all the constellations in the northern s-s-sky."

Hale mewed sadly and asked politely, "Please, Snake, can I have my tail back? I cannot play with my friends without it. My two tails help me balance along the long tightropes of the constellations and I hurt myself whenever I tumble. I haven't been able to catch up with my friends for the past two nights and I am starting to miss them dearly."

Snake's next reply frightened the poor little Comet Cat so badly that his whole body started to shake. "No!" Snake bellowed, his voice booming across the dark sky.

"Everyone else has-s-s one tail while I have none in the northern sky! You shouldn't be s-s-so greedy, you s-s-silly little Comet Cat. You should learn how to s-s-share. You only think about yourself and not the other stars-s-s around you. Everyone looks up at you as you chase the Hare, the Dove and the Crow across the sky with your two tails while no one notices me. Now you realise that my beautiful constellation is-s-s getting all the attention, you want it for yourself. S-s-so, you annoying, selfish Comet Cat, leave me alone and never come back!"

Hale ran away with his remaining tail between his legs. Had he really grown so greedy, he wondered. The cat ran and ran, too upset to look where he was going and that was when he tripped. He tumbled over one of the constellation's tightropes and plunged. Unable to stop himself, the poor little Comet Cat plummeted as a single-tailed shooting star, heading towards the land of Ia far below.

**

"I woke up and found the Northern Star hovering high above me. Your mother showed me the way," said Hale, ending his story.

"Mother led you to me?" I asked pointing to myself.

Hale blinked his green, diamond-shaped eyes once. A single tear ran down his furry cheek, shining brighter than the moon itself. The poor Comet Cat seemed very lonely, away from his friends who were high up in the night sky.

I stood up and said, "Hale, please don't be sad. I will help you get back to your friends."

"Really?" he asked with a sniff, rubbing his black button nose with his clawed paw.

I nodded. "Really, really. Now let's get your tail back, so you can return to the stars."

Chapter 4

Stranger on the Beach

"*E*bony?" It was a voice I had been longing to hear. As I ran to my balcony doors, I flung them open to find a flurry of white buffeting me. The snow whipped me with such power that I should have been ice cold, but instead I felt very warm. My skin tingled under the flakes. I felt something brush my leg and when I looked down there was Hale standing beside me. He mewed with an uncertain look in his green eyes. "It's okay," I told him. "It's only my mother."

As the two of us watched, the snow storm calmed and out she stepped, Stella Maris, the Northern Star, brightest of them all. She was even more beautiful than I remembered. The last time I saw her in human form was on the *Fire Crow*, the finest of all vessels travelling the ocean waves.

Mother still wore the same midnight-blue dress that I remembered so well. It gathered in little bunches, held in place by sparkling, star-like gemstones. Snowflakes fluttered down around her, melting the moment they touched the ground. Mine and Hale's mouths were open in a wide 'O' as she guided me back inside. The flurry kept falling, but left no trace on the carpet, even a puddle. Mother moved so gracefully, each of her steps as quiet as the next.

Hale began to purr loudly, breaking the silence. He trotted around us, tail and stump held high in greeting, wobbling to and fro. He was truly in need of his other tail, I thought.

I watched my mother reach down and stroke him from head to tail. The cat's tiny back arched as his purr grew even louder. Mother picked him up in her arms and tickled him under his chin while he rubbed his cheek against hers. "Hello, little friend," she told Hale before kneeling and placing him down gently on my bedroom floor. As she looked up at me, our eyes met and we smiled at one another. "Ebony," she sighed happily. A couple of happy tears tumbled down her rosy cheeks as I fell into her open arms.

"Mother," I exclaimed. She hugged me tightly, as if I was the most precious thing in the whole of Ia. Stella Maris, the Northern Star, was here at last and I was so happy!

I buried my face in her long, reddish-brown hair, taking in her smell. The fragrance was like no other I had ever come across. It was amazing! I was instantly taken on a journey through the cosmos, across millions of stars, and past thousands of suns and a mesmerising array of colours, created by the clouds of cosmic dust. I did not want to let my mother go, but I knew she had come here for a reason and this time it was Hale. I needed her help to fulfil my promise to him – to get back his tail that had been stolen by the mean constellation Snake.

"You will need to be brave, little one," Mother told me, still holding me tightly. "Be as brave as you were when you helped Abigail."

Leaning back, I gazed up into her eyes that shone brightly. Dancing across them were the stars, suns and colours created by cosmic dust.

"Hale needs your help in retrieving his tail and you are the only one who can do it, sweetheart," Mother said.

"Can you get Snake to give Hale back his tail?" I asked.

She shook her head.

"But you live among the stars. I live down here on Ia. I bet you could," I pleaded.

Mother smiled, shaking her head once again. "Snake will not listen to me." She placed her hand on my cheek and I snuggled into it. "I know you, and even though you might not believe it now, you do have the power of the stars, the strength of Ia itself and the courage of your father deep inside you."

Sighing, Mother let her hand drop to her side. I lurched forwards again, wrapping my arms around her in a tight hug. I didn't like to see her sad. She held me closer, rested her chin on the top of my head and whispered, "Be brave, my little Star Pirate."

"I will," I whispered back and she kissed me on the cheek.

"I have sent word to your father," she told me as she stood up, our hands still clasped in each other's.

"Father is coming here?" I cried out excitedly.

Mother shook her head. "Sadly, no, he's busy with his duties elsewhere in the kingdom, but he sends you his best man for the job."

I was disappointed that Captain Blake could not come, but I understood. He was a captain and one of the protectors of Ia, after all. I wondered who he had sent instead.

"You will need to go down to where the grounds of Ladon Manor meet the water's edge," Mother told me.

"But I promised Grandfather and Bea that I will never leave the grounds," I replied, looking down at Hale and he up at me. How was I ever going to help him if I could not go where I needed to?

Mother rubbed my fingers with her thumbs, comforting me. I looked up and found that she was smiling. I couldn't help but give a small grin back.

"I think this one time they will forgive you, love. They will know that you are being looked after by me." She pointed to her star, which was shining high above the gardens. It glowed a soft blue tonight, making it stand out from all those around it. "The boat will arrive shortly to take you safely to the Isle of the Spirits," she told me.

Stella Maris, the Northern Star, then looked to where Hale stood beside me. As I glanced down I saw his fur was standing on end.

"The Island of the Dead?" he hissed.

I gasped, my mouth hanging open in a very large 'O'. "Dead?" I gasped, making my mother chuckle.

53

"It is not as bad as it sounds," she replied. "The spirits walking the island are at peace and will not bother you, little one. Unlike Abigail, they cannot be seen by the living."

"Oh," I said.

My mother laughed again and nodded towards the Comet Cat. "I think your friend here is more concerned over who guards the gates between Ia and the night sky. You will need to seek out Canius Major, the Dog Star. You will find him in the valley where the stars' reflections fall. You will need to convince him to let you pass his gates and travel across the Milky Way. There, you will be able to locate Snake and ask for Hale's tail back."

The Comet Cat and I looked at one another, and then nodded. We were determined to succeed.

"I am truly sorry, my darling, for asking so much of you once again," said my mother, "but you are the only one who can do this task."

I looked up at her, our hands still clasped. The Star Bear in human form looked down at me with kind eyes. "You will understand one day, my darling. When you are older, you will understand." She looked sad and I didn't understand why. "Remember that your father and I are very proud of you, our little Star Pirate. I know you will try your very best for this little Comet Cat. It is important for him to be whole once again, for he too has an important task ahead of him."

Mother now glanced at Hale, the stars in her eyes sparkling more brightly than ever before. The cat's expression reflected my own as his mouth hung open in a very large 'O'.

I hugged my mother one last time before saying goodbye. Turning to Hale, she told him, "Look after my daughter for me. She is the most precious thing in my existence."

The Comet Cat blinked once slowly with his green diamond eyes.

"Goodbye, my sweet Ebony, and good luck to you both. I will be watching," said my mother.

In a blazing ball of white light, she was gone. The only sign that she had ever been there were a few glistening flakes of snow. Slowly, one by one, they tumbled to the floor. Hale and I watched them in complete silence. As they touched the rug they melted, making a faint sizzling sound. The quiet was broken when Hale eventually stated, "I don't like dogs." It made me giggle.

***

All was quiet as we waited on the beach. It reached far out into the distance, hugging the edge of the lands belonging to Ladon Manor, where I lived with my grandfather. Mother's star shone brightly above, making the sand turn all shades of blue and purple. Hale and I waited for the help my parents were sending to take us to the Isle of the Spirits. I preferred this name to the one my new friend, Hale, had called it. The spirits were at peace, Mother said. They were not the walking dead, but the ghosts of those who had passed away. Echoes of the long lost.

"There!" Hale cried out, bouncing up and down on his tiptoes. His speckled belly glittered strangely in the starlight.

"Where?" I asked excitedly.

"Beneath your mother's star," he said. "My eyesight is better than yours, but you should be able to see the plume of smoke."

Then I spotted it, just as the cat had said. Underneath my mother's star a plume of smoke rose from the horizon. I started jumping up and down too, waving my arms wildly in the air. "Maybe my father changed his mind! Maybe he has come in the *Fire Crow* after all."

But it was not the *Fire Crow* that was tugging closer to the shore. No, the boat ploughing through the tide was much smaller. As it neared, I could see that it was like the one I rowed with my father to Misty's cave. Instead of oars, circular paddles were positioned along both sides. In the middle was a chimney even bigger than me, billowing smoke. Its little belly ploughed through the white-crested waves as it clawed its way closer and closer to where Hale and I stood.

As the boat carved its way into the shoreline, a giant figure jumped over the side. His boots sank deeply into the wet sand, making a strange fizzing sound as steam rose all around him. What I saw next made me want to turn and run the other way – a giant with two heads! One was hooded, very large and sat on a very broad neck while the other was on top of a neck much skinnier than my own. This could not be my father's best man. He had to be an impostor!

I started to shake, but I did not sprint away, for I was the daughter of the land, sea and stars. I was a Star Pirate and whoever heard of such a person running away? Hale meowed and leapt up into my arms. The strange giant with steam rising from his feet shook the broader of his two heads.

"Who are you?" I called out to the figure. "I am Ebony Night, granddaughter of Rufus Night, lord of Ladon Manor, and these are his lands. I demand to know who you are!"

I could feel Hale swinging his head back and forth, looking up at me and then back at the stranger. The strange figure with the two heads chuckled, making his shoulders jolt up and down. "I know who you are, little missy," he replied.

My head tilted to one side. I recognised his voice, but where had I heard it before? "D-do I know y-you?" I asked the dark figure.

"I do hope so," he answered. "Hold on." The stranger with two heads took two steps forward. I readied myself to run all the way back to the safety of the manor with Hale in my arms, but the giant held up his hands, gesturing me to wait.

"Let's go," whispered the Comet Cat. "Maybe this wasn't the man your father sent. We can go and wait at the other end of the beach."

Shaking my head a little, I whispered back, "No. Wait."

We watched the giant reach down to his heel where there was a slight glow. I stroked Hale's black coat, for he was shaking with fear. In one swift movement the stranger lit a match. "Now do you recognise us?" he asked, pulling down his hood and holding the glowing stick in front of his face.

"Yes!" I answered excitedly, bouncing on the balls of my feet before running over to the giant and giving him a very large Star Bear hug.

Hale, who could now see why the stranger had appeared to have two heads, leapt from my arms and started to lick his paws, pretending he had not been scared in the first place.

The giant bent down to meet me. He was neither a stranger nor a giant with two heads, but a friend, or should I say friends? This was the pirate I had met long ago on a shingled beach. He lived in a hut much too small for him, surrounded by a white picket fence.

On his shoulder sat the most magnificent bird I had ever seen: Scarlett, the Fire Crow. These birds were bright red with two tails. One was fan-like, swishing open and closed over two of the most beautiful feathers, which were long and fluffy. On the end of each one was a staring red and white eye. No, these two were not unwelcome along these shores.

The giant pirate chuckled as he lifted me up to give me a giant Star Bear hug in return. My arms barely reached around his broad neck. "Hello, Ebony," he said, his smile just about visible through his dark beard. I noticed a few of his teeth missing, but I didn't mind.

"Hello erm…" I leant back to smile at him. "I'm sorry," I apologised, stroking Scarlett, who still sat high on the pirate's shoulder.

"Whatever for, little missy?" he asked as he put me back down on the sand.

"Last time we met, I never asked you your name," I answered.

The giant pirate chuckled. His shoulders bobbed up and down, jolting Scarlett, but she clung on. "Bob Macy," he told me, taking off his floppy hat and swinging it around in a funny kind of bow.

I smiled. "Hello, Bob Macy."

"And hello again, Ebony Night," he replied, grinning through his matted beard.

***

Just like the *Fire Crow*, this boat was steam-powered. However, it could not hold many more than the three of us. Bob Macy, the giant pirate with a magical boot, did not need to paddle. He didn't need to do anything apart from steer the little steam boat.

"How did my father send word to you?" I asked him curiously. I was holding Hale tightly in my arms.

He tucked his head, framed by the wispy whiskers, underneath my arm as he was not keen to be on water. I was not afraid. The water was my home as much as the land and stars above.

"Via Scarlett here," the pirate told me, patting the bright red bird on the head with one of his giant hands as he steered further out to sea with the other. "Fire Crows are clever anyway, but Scarlett is one of the very best. These birds have the ability to find anything on land or out at sea. I taught her to locate your father, Captain Blake. You see, she has learnt to come back and forth between us. If your father wishes to send me a message, he can do so quickly," he explained. "Clever, eh?"

I nodded, looking up admiringly at Scarlett, the Fire Crow.

The Comet Cat wailed as he wiggled in my arms. "Are we there yet?" he enquired and I shook my head. He groaned again and shoved his head further beneath my arm.

"Your friend doesn't look very well," Bob remarked.

"Do you know how long it will be until we reach the island?" I asked, looking down at the Comet Cat.

"Not long, maybe half an hour."

Again, Hale wailed loudly in my arms.

"If that," Bob added with a worried look on his face.

Chapter 5

The Dog Star

W hen we arrived on the shores of the Isle of the Spirits, Bob Macy did not stick around for long. "No one has set foot on this isle since your mother's time," he told me. "I will make a quick exit, little missy, out of respect for the dead, if you don't mind. I will return at dawn."

I nodded, unsure of what else to say.

"I wish you the best of luck and hope you find whatever you are looking for," he added. With that, Bob Macy pushed his little steam boat back out to sea and was gone.

High above, my mother's star shone brightly, lighting up the northern sky and the land below in a bluish hue. Around us there was nothing apart from sand to the side, the sea behind and overgrown woodland in front. "Now where?" I asked aloud.

Suddenly, Hale leapt out of my arms and started to run very fast towards the woodland. "Ebony, can you hear them?" he called back.

I ran after the little Comet Cat, whose speckled

belly shone dimly in the forest. We crashed loudly through the undergrowth. "Hear who?" I yelled out.

"The stars!" he replied.

I ran as fast as I could, but Hale was much quicker than me. Soon he was out of sight. The dark wood cut out any source of light that my mother was sending us. I could not see the stars or Hale. Feeling very alone, I stood still, looking as hard as I could for any sign of the Comet Cat. He was nowhere to be seen, but what I could hear was a strange sound indeed. From the distance came a sort of tinkling, as if someone was running their fingers along some chimes. Was this what Hale heard? Was it really the stars?

I began to run once again, the trees and bushes catching my pyjamas. I had remembered to put on my shoes for this adventure, which was lucky, because as I made my way towards the strange noise, I splattered through many muddy puddles left by the rain the night before. Strict Bea will not be pleased at the state of me, I thought.

I burst through the undergrowth and into a clearing only to trip, and I found myself tumbling through the long grass. When I looked back to see what I had fallen over, I spotted Hale. He was just sitting there, as still as a statue, his green diamond eyes open wide.

"Hale!" I called, walking up to him with my arms crossed, just like Strict Bea did when she told me off. "There you are! Why did you run off and leave me? I thought I'd lost you…" My voice faded away as I noticed he was not moving at all.

The Comet Cat did not even twitch a whisker or wiggle an ear, and I realised he was frozen with fear. Had I frightened him? "I'm sorry," I said, brushing his head, which was slightly too big for his body. Then my own eyes grew wide. The drumming in my ears had come back, along with the feeling to escape, to run.

Someone was breathing down the back of my neck. I spun around, but much too quickly, lost my footing and fell, landing on the soft grass with a muffled thump. What I saw standing in front of me made me yelp loudly. A giant black nose and very long fangs were much too close to my face. I backed up a little to be beside Hale. We both shook from head to toe with fear.

"Who dares enter these lands?" the creature demanded. "These are the lands of the spirits. The lands of the stars who guide lost souls to their rightful place. Speak now or you will feel our wrath!"

"Our?" I thought aloud, curiosity overwhelming my fear. As I looked, I saw that the black nose and fangs were not the only black nose and fangs. There were three sets of them! I now understood why Hale was so scared. It was not because of me telling off the little Comet Cat after all. It was this creature that had frightened him. Not only did it have three heads, but it was also a giant dog!

One head was yellow with white flecks and in the darkness it shone so much brighter than the other two that it hurt my eyes. In the middle was the largest of the three heads and it was pure white with eyes burning the most magnificent hue of blue I had ever seen.

The third one matched the night so perfectly that it was hard to make out the creature's head at all. Only when the head moved or breathed out, causing ripples of vapour to shift slightly in the light from Mother's star, could I see its outline. This head might have been the darkest and most mysterious of all three, but it made me sweat. This dog's breath made tonight feel like a baking hot summer's day!

"Speak!" The pure white head snapped its teeth

together an inch away from my face, his fangs flashing in the light from its sibling. The air reverberated with the dog's growls.

"My n-name," I gulped. "My n-name is Ebony Night," I began.

The ears of the yellow head twitched. It nudged its brother, the white head, and to my amazement the dog backed up a few steps. The third head snorted disapprovingly, however. His mottled black-and-blue coat, which matched the night so perfectly, rippled madly. "Stand!" it commanded and I did.

I felt the Comet Cat move beside me and I caught him as he leapt into my arms, hissing at the creature. "Shush, Hale, it'll be alright," I said, stroking his black coat.

All three heads watched me closely as I took a moment to comfort the little cat. Out of the corner of my eye, I saw the middle one gaze up at the Northern Star for a few moments before looking back at me. His brothers' eyes never left mine.

"I am Sirius," the dog's middle head told me. "I am the axle, the counterbalance between my brothers. I am the judge and my judgement is final. My brother here is Mirzam," Sirius added, looking at the head to the right whose colours blended so perfectly with the darkness. "He is considered to be the quickest to judge and it takes a lot to change his mind about anything or anyone."

A horrifying growl made Mirzam's jowls quiver, a flash of teeth gnashing in the night air.

"It is true, brother, and I only speak the truth," said Sirius. He then nodded to the yellow head on his left. "And this is my other brother, Wezen. No one, apart from the stars, can look at him for long periods of time. He is the deep thinker, the observer, and together we are Canis Major, the Dog Star."

I glanced from one brother to the other, unsure what to make of the three. Mirzam was breathing heavily. With every growl his jowls rippled, making his whole face more noticeable in the night light. I turned away from him to Sirius whose eyes glittered, boring into my own. He said his judgement was final, but what did he mean? What judgement?

Finally, I glanced at Wezen, the brightest of all three brothers. I looked into his eyes, which, I was surprised to find, were as black as the fur of his brother, Mirzam. Wezen's eyes were the only part of him I could bare to look at.

"Why are you here?" asked Sirius. "Speak now, as Mirzam is becoming very impatient. While Wezen has decided we should hear what you have to say, I am the axle, the counterbalance, the final judgment. Hurry, we have not eaten for a whole century and I may just agree with my brother, Mirzam, and say we gobble you both up. "

The third and darkest of the heads growled impatiently. With the heat that rolled off him, I felt like I was standing in a steamship's boiler room.

"My friend, Hale, is a twin-tailed C-comet Cat," I began shakily. "One of his tails has been taken by the constellation known as Snake. Hale let him borrow it for a little while, so Snake could be recognised down here on Ia. Ia's people didn't realise he was a snake until Hale helped him, because Snake's tail is in the southern sky, not the north. Now Snake won't give Hale his tail back, so I've come here to ask for it."

"Why doesn't Hale ask for it back himself?" asked Wezen.

His voice was kind and song-like. I liked him and

couldn't help but give a small smile in his direction. "He did, but Hale is too polite to stand up to Snake," I replied.

"Then why did he come to you?" Sirius asked me.

I was about to answer when I was surprised to hear Hale's little voice say, "Because I fell." He sounded ashamed, but I didn't know why. Even Mirzam stopped growling and watched the Comet Cat most carefully.

"Ebony has been very kind and generous enough to offer me her help," Hale explained. "Her mother, Stella Maris, Navigator of the Sea, helped guide me to her. Her father, Captain Blake of the steamship *Fire Crow*, also helped by sending one of his best men to bring us here tonight. When I fell, I felt lost and alone. I am a Comet Cat and I should be in the night sky, running the tightropes of the constellations and playing chase with the Hare, the Dove and the Crow across the night sky. But then Ebony became my friend. She helped me without asking for anything in return, just like a best friend would."

I looked down at Hale. I never thought I would find another friend like Misty, but here he was. This brave little cat was standing up for me against this giant, three-headed Dog Star.

"Please don't eat her," Hale pleaded, his voice squeaking slightly higher than normal. "Eat me instead. She came here because of me and I don't want her to be eaten."

Tears rolled down my face and I watched in horror as Canis Major, the Dog Star, stepped forwards. Each of the heads licked their chops, drool dripping from their long fangs, as they stepped closer and closer to my new best friend. I watched in horror as Hale jumped from my arms, ready to meet Canis Major head-on.

The cat, with a head that was too big for his body and framed by wispy whiskers, looked tiny compared to the massive Dog Star. He was the bravest Comet Cat I would ever know.

"No!" I yelled, running forwards to place myself between Canis Major and Hale. "You can't eat him!" Even though I was shaking, I refused to move. I turned to the little cat and he looked up at me, his eyes full of surprise. "You're my best friend too," I told him.

74

Without caring what happened to me, I bent down and hugged Hale once more as we waited to be gobbled up, but as the seconds passed, nothing happened. Turning slowly, I was surprised to find Canis Major, the Dog Star, sitting there watching us and wagging his tail!

"Told you," Wezen said to his brothers smugly.

"I still don't think she is worthy enough to cross the Milky Way," Mirzam remarked.

Sirius spoke loudly over his brother's judgments: "Silence, brothers."

The Dog Star rose, as did I, holding Hale tightly in my arms. I tried not to cry any more. I was a Star Pirate after all.

"Ebony Night, daughter of Stella Night, the Northern Star, and of Captain Blake of the steamship *Fire Crow*, we grant you permission to pass our gates and enter the Milky Way, in order to retrieve your friend's tail from the Constellation known by the name of Snake," announced Sirius. "We do not, however, guarantee your safety. Once you pass these gates, you are on your own."

Nodding, I said, "I understand." After a few moments' hesitation, I added, "Thank you," before curtseying to the three heads. In return, all three bowed, even Mirzam.

"You should not thank us," Wezen said. "You have shown that you would give up your life for this young Comet Cat and bravery is greatly honoured here. No one has entered these lands and lived to tell the tale, apart from your own mother many years ago. These lands are meant to be a resting place for the dead before they cross over. Only those living souls who prove themselves worthy enough will we given safe passage. Yet only one of you may pass."

Sirius then turned to speak to Hale. "Be warned, Comet Cat, if you do not return to the sky by the night's end, you will be forever stranded here on Ia. Your powers cannot protect you from this doom."

"Good luck," Wezen whispered to us before Canis Major turned and entered the dark wood.

Hale and I watched as the Dog Star's light faded into the night. Once the creature was gone, we took in our surroundings. "Wow!" we gasped together.

Before us lay a bowl-shaped valley and through its centre ran a dark river. This was no ordinary river for its waters flowed from the clouds in the sky, which were of all kinds of colours, like a rainbow. In the starlight they changed and shimmered. Where the water met the ground below, tiny droplets billowed out into the air, which were just as colourful. As they tumbled to the ground, they twinkled strangely, joining in with the melody of the stars.

Just below the waterfall was a dark, deep pool, from which the river flowed out towards the ocean that lay beyond the surrounding woodland. Reflecting on the calm surface, I could see the cosmos: a million stars, a thousand suns and a mesmerising array of coloured clouds of dust. I then remembered my mother's eyes. Was this what she had been trying to show me earlier? On either side of the waterfall stood two large pillars, just like the ones at the entrance to Ladon Manor, but instead of the Star Bears at home, the mighty three-headed Dog Star was carved on the top.

"These must be the gates Canis Major was talking about," I whispered to Hale and he nodded. Looking at the distance between the river and the black-blue heavens above, I asked, "I take it the river is the only way up?" I guessed he would know the ways of the stars as he was a Comet cat after all. Hale nodded again.

Raising my eyes up to the constellation Snake, I could see Hale's tail glistening brightly in the night sky. "I just hope I can get back before dawn."

"You will," the cat told me. "I trust you."

I tore my eyes away from Snake to look down at Hale. He grinned, his tiny fangs glistening in the starlight. He reminded me of the time I saw my mother transform into her Star Bear form. When she smiled, her long, sharp teeth glistened like that too.

Smiling kindly at my new best friend, I told him, "I will miss you."

The little Comet Cat placed his two paws on my chest, bumped his nose with mine and replied, "I will miss you too, friend."

For a little while longer we sat together, Hale and I, as we watched the tightrope of the constellations rise higher in the glistening sky.

Chapter 6
Reflections

T he starlit river was freezing! It looked so still along the riverbank that I was surprised to find the water rushing past me when I jumped in. I had to swim very fast to stay in one place. And I really did not know how on Ia I was going to swim all the way up into the sky!

"Believe in yourself," Hale called to me over the roar of the water. "I don't know much about the powers of this island, but I do know that if you don't believe, you won't be able to reach the top."

Glancing at the never-ending waterfall once again, I swallowed and then nodded to the Comet Cat, who was watching me from the riverbank. I knew he was worried about me. "Here goes," I said, and with all my might I began to swim towards the roaring, starry waterfall.

I was getting closer to the pillars where the carving of Canis Major, the Dog Star, sat on top. The sky water thundered on to the ground, lashing down into the deep, dark pool where the reflections of the stars collided. I was nearly there, but my arms and legs were tiring. How was I ever going to climb all that way?

Unexpectedly, I found myself going backwards and I started to panic. My limbs were growing heavier and the dark, cold water was getting into my mouth. I tried to reach for the riverbank, but it was too far away now. I was not strong enough – I was going to drown. I screamed, "Help!"

"Ebony!"

I turned my head to see Hale running alongside me as I was swept down the fast-flowing river. "Keep swimming!" he meowed at me loudly.

"I'm trying!" I called back, but the current was too strong. The water was splashing over my head now and I could not keep afloat. My arms and legs were getting heavier.

How was I meant to swim all the way up to the waterfall, and then up to the starry sky? How was I meant to find my way across the Milky Way, discover the constellation Snake and then convince him to give back Hale's tail? And all before the sun rose?

"This task is impossible," I mumbled as I sank beneath the inky black waters.

***

I could not see anything but black water. Above the roar of the river, I heard a strange fizzing, popping sound. I was shaking, freezing cold. However, I was no longer wet. A circular wall of water surrounded me. Looking up through this wall I saw pinpricks of light – the stars shimmering way above my head. From here everything and everyone seemed so very far away. I was stuck.

"I am alone!" I cried out, remembering the words of the blonde girl's brother.

"No, you're not," said a very soft voice.

"Who? Who's there?" I asked between hiccups.

"Me."

A little white light appeared in front of me.

"And me," said another small voice as a similar light appeared.

"And me."

"And don't forget me."

Soon there were dozens and dozens of little sparks of light all the way round me. They reminded me of the stars in the night sky. I felt better, slightly warmer and not so alone.

"Who are you?" I asked.

"We are the Reflections. Watch!"

In front of my very eyes one of the lights changed into Hale, the Comet Cat. "We can transform into anything that is reflected in the water," it told me.

"Can you turn into me?" I asked, but the Reflection shook its head. "You are in the water and have no reflection here. The little Comet Cat is looking for you, so we can copy him easily. We can also copy the stars, and anything or anyone that is reflected in the water."

The little lights gathered around the Reflection that was now the copy Comet Cat and whispered in his ear. Then it asked me, "We were curious to find someone in our waters and wondered why you are so upset?"

I told them Hale's story: how he lost his tail and found me, the encounter with the Dog Star, and how he allowed me to pass through his gates. "But now I am stuck," I added. "I need to go all the way up to the stars and retrieve Hale's tail before the sun rises, or else he will never be able to go back among the constellations to play with the Hare, the Dove and the Crow. Hale told me to believe I can do it, but the task is impossible."

"I believe in you," said one Reflection, sounding like my mother, Stella Maris, the Northern Star.

"I believe in you," another told me in the voice of Sirius.

"I believe in you," said a version of Wezen.

"I believe in you," called out the remainder of the Reflections in a mixture of tones.

"And I, too, believe in you," added the Reflection of Hale.

I gazed around at all of them, my mouth hanging open in a very large 'O'. Then I turned back to the little copy Comet Cat and asked, "You do?"

He nodded. "We not only reflect the way someone appears or sounds, but also the way they feel."

I smiled. "Thank you. Then I believe I can do this too."

The little copy Comet Cat smiled back. Suddenly, I found myself floating. Slowly, I rose off the riverbed and up through the wall of water, the currents no longer battering me here and there. I was rising towards the glittering surface, gradually at first and then more quickly.

"Thank you!" I called out again, laughing as I waved down at the Reflections that were now so far away as to be tiny spots of light. The one of Hale smiled, waving at me with his little clawed paw before shimmering back into his original form.

"Bye, Ebony," the Reflections called out as one.

"Bye," I replied in a hushed whisper, for I was very sad to be leaving the curious little lights behind.

I looked up to see the shimmering stars above, the brightest of all being my mother. Kicking as hard as I could, I broke the water's surface. Instantly, I heard my name: "Ebony!"

I turned my head and there he was, the real Hale, with his speckled belly and a head that was slightly too big for his body, framed by all those wispy whiskers.

"Hale!" I called back.

The Comet Cat ran to keep up as the torrent pushed me up river. "Thank you!" I yelled.

"What for?" he asked breathless.

I rushed past the gates with the carving of Canis Major on top. Realising that I was fast approaching the deep, dark pool where the roaring waters met the ground below, I looked back at Hale. He stopped just outside the gates as I was the only one whom the Dog Star had allowed to pass through.

"For believing in me," I called back, amazed to find myself being carried up the roaring waterfall. I didn't even need to kick my legs.

"Of course I believed in you, silly!" Hale laughed as he watched me rise higher and higher, up into the night sky, unable to join me.

The water was not even cold any more, but warm, as if I was in a steaming, hot bath back at home, but drier. "See you soon, Hale," I replied. "I'll bring back your tail for you, I promise."

As I waved to the Comet Cat far below, the water took me over the top of the falls and up on to the rainbow clouds.

Chapter 7

The Final Judgement

*A*s I rose through the rainbow clouds, the vapours cleared and I found myself on a walkway. *If this is the Milky Way, it is spectacular!* Above me was a range of coloured cosmic dust, streaking across the night sky. Thousands upon thousands of tiny stars shone brightly, like little pinholes in a thick blanket. The walkway was see-through with streaks of frosting here and there. I looked down and was pleased to see nothing but swirling rainbow cloud beneath my feet.

Suddenly, there was a flare of light overhead, but when I looked up it vanished. There was nothing but a multitude of colours streaking across the black sky and thousands of tiny stars twinkling so high, singing their mesmerising melody.

As I started walking down the Milky Way, once again the light appeared, but this time it stayed. I looked up and above me was a Comet Cat looking just like Hale!

"Hale?" I asked.

"No," the little black cat replied. "I am his older brother, Bopp."

"Brother?" I mouthed.

The cat bobbed his head. Now that I looked more closely, I noticed how he looked different. Bopp had blue diamond-shaped eyes and white wisps of fur around his collar. The white made his head look even bigger than Hale's. Bopp's fluffy tail had a white tip, whereas Hale's was all inky black.

"That's right. I haven't seen my brother for a while. I thought I saw Snake with his tail last night. Am I mistaken?" Bopp was looking at me with his big blue eyes. He came down and sat on the frosty

89

Milky Way, watching me closely, while I told him how his brother had lost his tail and of our adventure so far.

"So, Mother sent me to help Hale by asking for his tail back. She believes I am the only one who can do it. I hope I can get it back in time or else your brother won't be able to return to the stars," I added.

"I am sure you will. Shall I show you the way?" Bopp asked me, getting up and stretching his long, sleek legs.

"Oh yes, please!" I replied.

Bopp grinned widely, his fangs flashing in the starlight. "This way!"

I followed as quickly as I could as the Comet Cat half-trotted, half-glided down the icy path, his bushy black tail with the white tip held high in the air.

"Is it far?" I asked after a while.

The only sound I could hear was the faint, tinkling melody of the stars surrounding us on all sides. I could no longer see the rainbow clouds beneath my feet. The waterfall and Hale were far behind. Luckily, the frosty walkway was not so see-through as to make my head spin. The stars above swirled and danced around one another playfully. The home of my mother, Hale and all the other constellations was truly magical. No wonder my friend wanted to return.

"Not far," Bopp replied to my question.

High above, I saw shooting stars zoom across the sky. "Are those your brothers and sisters?" I asked as I jogged beside Bopp, trying to keep up. He shook his large head, framed by its white mane. "Some of them are my brothers and sisters, but others are friends."

"Are all shooting stars Comet Cats?" I questioned.

Again, Bopp shook his bushy mane. "Not all are small cats. Some of the comets are larger than me, Hale, and my other brothers and sisters. There are tigers, lions, cheetahs, jaguars and even leopards."

Seeing my confusion, he added, "Many of the creatures have been extinct down on Ia for many years and others are dying out even as we speak. Sadly, what happens on Ia is reflected in the heavens, and many of the larger species of shooting stars are becoming very rare indeed, though, thankfully, us Comet Cats are not."

"I've heard that before," I replied, thinking hard. "What happens on Ia is reflected in the heavens… or was it the other way around? My grandfather said it a lot when he told me stories about my mother."

Bopp bobbed his head. "It is true. Each realm balances the other."

I jogged beside the cat open-mouthed, which made him chuckle. "You'll catch Star Flies in that mouth if you keep it open like that," he told me, winking.

"So, what if I am unable to return Hale's tail to him in time?" I asked.

Again, Bopp shook his head, flapping his mane from side to side. "I do not know what will happen. The imbalance will need a counteraction somehow." Suddenly, he stopped trotting beside me and announced, "This is where you need to hold on." He turned, showing me his fluffy tail.

I gasped. "You mean your tail?"

The Comet Cat bobbed his head. "If you want to reach Snake's head in time, you need to trust me." He smiled kindly, so I nodded and grabbed his tail. "Hold on tight," he told me, and before I knew it, we lurched off into the starry sky.

Bopp's tail grew longer and longer until it resembled the shooting stars I had seen from my bedroom window, back at Ladon Manor. At first I was afraid that I would let go and fall, crashing on to the ground far below, so I closed my eyes tightly.

After a little while I came to realise where I was. This was my mother's home – the starry heavens that I could see so high above Ia from my bedroom window – and now I was part of it, flying through the cosmos with a shooting star, so I should not be afraid. I opened one eye, then the other. I was flying through the kingdom of the stars!

Bopp was pulling me along at a super-fast speed. It… was… AMAZING! I laughed out loud. The cat turned his head and joined in.

"Having fun back there?" he enquired and I nodded.

"Want to go faster?" he asked and after a moment's hesitation I nodded again. Bopp grinned. "Right then, you asked for it!"

I swallowed as I watched the cat's little legs run on the spot before he zoomed straight up in a streak of rainbow-coloured light. "Whaaaaaa!" I yelled at the top of my lungs, making the nearby constellations turn their giant heads. They stared at us wide-eyed as we passed them by in a ball of light, but soon I was yelling, "Weeeeee!"

As we did a loop-the-loop, I laughed and so did Bopp, the Comet Cat, with the large head framed by a floppy, white mane. He bobbed and weaved between the tightropes of the constellations. "You're so fast," I commented. I was smiling from ear to ear.

"Wait until Hale gets his tail back. He's even faster than me. Hold on, we've got to go a bit higher and then we'll be there."

We shot straight up to the twinkling stars high above. I held on with one hand as I waved down at the other constellations left far behind. They waved back, slowly. "Byeeeee!" I called out to them, laughing.

"Bye," they replied. Their deep, booming voices would have woken any slumbering stars from their sleep.

***

Bopp levelled out as he flew alongside an almighty high wall. It was silver and very, very scaly. Its surface shone brightly. As we levelled up beside it, the night sky beyond was blocked out.

"What is this?" I asked as the Comet Cat zoomed in and out alongside the wall with ease.

"Not what, but who," he corrected me. "This is Snake."

My breath caught in my throat. Without looking back at me, Bopp nodded. "He stretches from the southern to the northern sky, and he's very large for a snake. I wish you luck, Ebony Night. To get back, Hale's tail will not be easy."

The Comet Cat's pace slowed down as he turned left and then right, following Snake's giant form northward. "And this is where we must part for now," he told me sadly as he finally came to a complete stop.

I found myself standing on another strange walkway. This time it was more like a cobweb of silvery thread. "The tightropes that Hale told me about," I gasped, looking at the walkway in awe.

I let go of the cat's tail and as I did so, it shrank down to its regular size and bushiness. "It was nice meeting you, Bopp," I told him. "I will try my hardest to bring your brother back in time."

Bopp, with his oversized head and floppy white mane, smiled at me. Bowing his head slightly, he said, "I know you will, and I am sure your mother chose the right person for the job."

"Thank you, Bopp."

"You are very welcome, little Star Pirate, and good luck." In a flash of bright white light, Bopp, the little Comet Cat, was gone.

Chapter 8

Snake's Heart

I was scared and I mean really, really scared. Shaking on the spot, I jumped as Snake's body slithered slightly.

"Who is-s-s there?" His voice echoed through the cosmos, sounding angry. "Who is-s-s there?" Snake boomed once again, more impatiently this time. His silvery, scaly body moved. His rippling muscles made it sound like rain was about to cascade down on us.

I knew I had to answer him, so I swallowed. "Eb…" My voice trailed away to nothing. I bit my lip. Taking another deep breath, I tried again. "Ebony Night," I said, quickly adding, "Sir." Grandfather always told me the way to deal with difficult clients was to be really polite to them.

"S-S-Sir?" Snake's voice did not sound irritated or annoyed any more. "Well, Mis-s-s Night, please step forward and present yourself."

I took a few deep breaths. I needed to get Hale's tail back and time was running out fast. As I balanced along the tightrope, being careful not to fall off, I started wondering how I was going to do this. I knew that winning Hale's tail back was not going to be easy, otherwise Mother would have done it herself. *What did I know that my mother didn't?*

For once, I was thankful for Grandfather and his long, boring talks about work. His voice popped up inside my head: "Never show your fear, Ebony. That is the key to success when you are dealing with a tricky customer. They can sense it."

Sense it? What an odd thing to say.

I stood up straight and took the last few steps to reveal myself to Snake himself. I imagined taking all my fears and locking them away in a tiny box. Now was not the time to be frightened. I was the daughter of the land, sea and stars after all. My mother was Stella Maris, the Northern Star and Navigator of the Sea. I was the daughter of Captain Blake, and the three of us together were the Protectors of Ia. I was also the granddaughter of the best businessman Ia had ever known.

And, most importantly, tonight I was going to be the best friend to Hale, the Comet Cat who fell from the night sky. Tonight I was going to get his tail back!

As I rounded Snake's body, his head lifted from his nest of tightropes. They groaned under his enormous weight. "S-s-so," said the giant constellation. "You are Ebony Night, yes-s-s?"

"Yes, sir."

His crystal eyes looked at me from high above with an ice-cold stare.

"You flatter me, why?" Snake asked sharply.

"Flatter, sir?" I tilted my head. "I was merely brought up to show manners to my elders."

"Manners-s-s? Manners are so hard to come by these days-s-s," Snake hissed, moving his massive, scaly form. Some of the tightropes snapped and all too soon I realised his upper body was curling around me! The rest of him continued to sliver over the horizon. This snake was big!

Before I could think, he picked me up in his coiled upper body. "You're not from around here, are you?"

I shook my head. Snake was squashing me so tightly in his enormous, glittering body that I was finding it hard to breathe.

"Are you?" he bellowed, his forked tongue lashing at my hair.

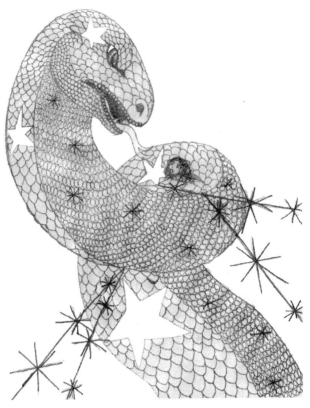

"No. Sir," I managed to say.

"That's better." Snake gave a sharp nod of his diamond-shaped head and set me back down on the tightropes again.

I was so happy to be able to breathe again.

"Why are you here?" he asked me.

My ribs ached so much from where he had been squashing me that I could not answer. Snake repeated the question. I saw him lick his scaly lips, eyeing me up as something good to eat. Out of the corner of my eye, I saw Mother's star wink at me. With her presence, I felt much braver.

Before he could gobble me up, I took a deep breath and answered his question: "I am daughter of Captain Blake of the steamship *Fire Crow*," I announced, sounding much braver than I felt. "I am daughter of Stella Night, also known as Stella Maris, the Northern Star, Navigator of the Sea."

Snake hissed suddenly. I could not work out why, but it reminded me of someone saying, "Shush!" I watched him raise his head northward. His never-blinking, ice-cold eyes glared up at my mother's star, which still shone brighter than any other in the night sky.

"S-s-she asked for the Comet Cat's tail back?" Snake began to hiss again, but this time it sounded much like laughter. "You have come to ask for it back?"

I stared up into those giant, crystal eyes as they turned on me now. I was not afraid. The box was no longer needed. "Yes," I said confidently, determined to succeed. Snake was a bully.

"You've wasted your time," he replied.

"I will not go back to Ia without it!" I insisted as I marched closer to Snake's scaly form. "Hale fell to Ia because of you. Because of you, he got lost. Because of you, Mother had to show him the way to me. And because of you, I gained a friend."

"S-s-so you gained a friend?" Snake repeated my words. "You s-s-see, I was right in taking that silly, show-off Comet Cat's tail after all."

Snake was laughing again through his hisses. "Hale thinks-s-s he's so popular, playing games with the Hare, the Dove and the Crow. They say he's the fastest of all the Comet Cats and now he is lost without his tail. Now he's the Fallen Comet Cat and will never set foot in the s-s-starry heavens again whereas I will become the Mighty Snake of the night sky!"

Snake became boastful, but what he did not realise was that I was beginning to understand why Mother said I was the only one able to get Hale's tail back.

Snake hissed more loudly than before, his neck arching higher and higher, with his head tucked into his shaking belly. He reminded me of the village children who held on to one another as they laughed at me. My mother was unable to get Hale's tail back because she had never been bullied. But I could, because I now understood why Snake was being so mean.

"You're lonely," I told him. I did not need to raise my voice to stand up to this bully.

Snake stopped laughing. His ice-cold eyes glared down at me. "I... am... what?" he snapped.

"You're lonely," I repeated. "That is why you are jealous of Hale."

Snake snapped the air in annoyance with his long fangs. "How dare you!" he bellowed, making my hair stream out behind me in a great whoosh. "How dare you accuse me of being jealous-s-s! You are a tiny, insignificant little girl. I should squash you where you stand!"

Snake's massive upper body coiled, towering high above me, but I did not move. I just smiled as I did not feel scared of this bully. It was Snake who was afraid now – afraid of the truth.

"But you won't," I told him. "You are lonely. You asked Hale to borrow his tail, so the people of Ia will look up at the night sky and recognise you for who you really are. Hale let you borrow it because he could see how much it meant to you. He trusted you. No one wants to be lonely, Snake, and when you took Hale's tail away from him, he couldn't keep up with his friends in their chasing game. He was the one who became lonely."

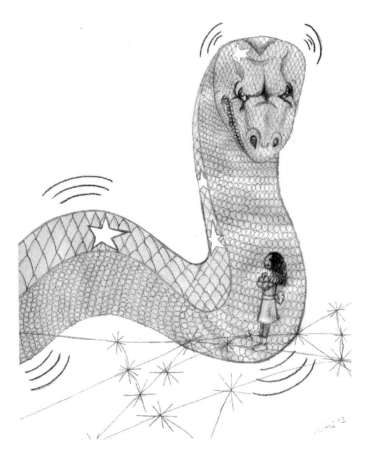

Snake still held his coiled body high above me, but I did not move an inch. His cold, crystal eyes glowed menacingly, but still I did not move.

"You turned Hale away when he asked you for help and in doing so you lost your only friend, who asked for nothing in return. Friends are meant to help one another, Snake. Help Hale now and give him back his tail. Don't lose the one true friend you had and become even lonelier than before."

A few seconds passed, during which neither of us moved or made a sound. The only noise was the twinkling melody of the stars dancing around us. Snake's unblinking, silver eyes bored deeper into my own brown, golden-flecked ones. Then, slowly, his body uncoiled, flopping back on to the tightrope beside me with a great thump.

I watched in wonder as his eyes turned from icy cold to a warm ocean blue. "You are right," he said sadly. Snake turned his head, tucking it into his body, and I realised he was ashamed of himself. "I was-s-s the greedy one," he admitted. "Hale, the little Comet Cat, helped me when no other would. He gave me his-s-s tail without as-s-sking for anything in return.

He was-s-s a true friend, even if I wasn't. Hold out your hand."

I did as he asked and Snake turned his head, reaching far back along his body. I wobbled slightly as the tightropes groaned under his shifting weight. As his upper half shifted back into view, he lowered his massive, scaly head to my eye level. Between his sharp, glistening fangs, he delicately held the rainbow-coloured, glittering tail of a comet. "Tell him I am s-s-sorry," said Snake, turning his now warm, ocean-blue eyes on me.

"I will," I replied.

Snake swung his head up high above me once again and nodded.

"Thank you, Snake. I am now your friend too," I told him and leaning forwards I hugged his warm, scaly belly.

Suddenly, a bright white light appeared under the spot where my head rested. I pulled away, unsure of where it might have come from.

"What did you do?" Snake asked, sounding alarmed. Lowering his head, he swished it back and forth, trying to get a better look at the light.

"I didn't do anything!" I answered.

The light shone brighter and brighter until it hurt too much for me to see. A wave of energy rolled over me and I was knocked off the tightrope on which I was standing.

"Ebony!" Snake bellowed my name and I heard a snap of his jaw, but he was too slow to catch me. I wailed as I fell, plummeting towards Ia at great speed. I covered my head with one arm while I held on to Hale's rainbow tail in my other hand. Then everything went black.

***

I opened my eyes and lifted my head a little. That was when I saw some gigantic paws, a panting, hairy chest and three heads looming over me. "Well done, Ebony Night!" It was Sirius, the middle head of the Dog Star, who spoke.

Looking around, I found that I was back on Ia, on the Isle of the Spirits, in one piece. "You managed to do what no other beings on Ia or even in our kingdom up in the starry heavens could achieve," Sirius said, drawing my attention back to the giant, three-headed Dog Star standing in front of me. "You have achieved your goal – you have made the Comet Cat known as Hale whole again."

I felt something brush my leg and looking down I saw him, his head framed by wispy whiskers and his speckled belly shining in the starlight. With fur all black and shiny, he held his tails up high. I did a double-take.

"Hale!" I cried out with tears tumbling down my rosy cheeks. "You've got your tail back!" As he leapt up into my arms, the Comet Cat nuzzled my face, bumping his nose against mine and purring very loudly.

"We told you once…"

Hale and I turned back to Canis Major and found it was Wezen who now spoke. "…that only those who prove themselves will we save," he concluded.

Wirzum nodded his head. "You have very much proven yourself to us, and to the rest of the constellations and their brethren, little Star Pirate," he told me. "You are truly the daughter of the Northern Star."

With that the three heads bowed in one fluid movement and vanished, along with the gateway to the Milky Way, as dawn poked its head over the treetops.

"It's morning!" I gasped.

Only now did I realise that the night sky was giving way to the rising sun. Above us the darkness was alive with pink, turquoise and pale yellow. I felt Hale's purring stop and as I faced him once again, I watched in horror as his second tail started to fade, but that was not the only change. The cat's entire form fizzled and transformed in front of my eyes. His head shrank to a slightly more normal size and the stars on his belly dulled to become plain, white specks.

"Oh, Hale, I am so sorry," I said, nuzzling him as I felt his starlight fading within him. "I told your brother, Bopp, that I would bring you back to him safely. I'm so sorry."

To my amazement the Comet Cat was chuckling.

"Why are you smiling at me like that?" I asked, rubbing my eyes.

"Because I chose to stay," he told me.

My mouth opened into a wide 'O'. "You did?"

Hale bobbed his head, reminding me so much of his older brother, Bopp, as he did so.

"You'll catch Star Flies if you keep your mouth open like that, you know?" he remarked, tapping my chin playfully with his paw.

"So I've been told," I said to the little Comet Cat, who now looked like an ordinary cat sitting in my arms. We smiled at one another in silence.

Then Hale told me, "Your mother came to me while you were gone. She told me that she had unbalanced the nature of Ia and the heavens by choosing a life in the stars. She chose to watch those on Ia from afar, to see you grow and turn into the brave little girl she sees before us now. Your mother knew you had the means to convince Snake, above all others, to give back my tail, and she also told me that I have an important part to play and that being here is important."

"What do you mean?" I asked.

Hale blinked up at me from where he sat in my arms. "Me being here," he replied. "I will help to correct the natural balance of the realms once again. Your mother was a human who chose to live with the stars. I am from the stars, but choose to live with the humans, with you down here, on Ia. Your mother promised that she would send word to my friends and family that I am safe. Ebony, you have helped me without asking for anything in return. You are truly a good friend and I want to stay here with you."

Staring at the little black cat, I asked, "Really?"

"Really, really," he replied and we grinned at one another.

I placed him down on the grassy ground. "But

what about your starlight? You look just like an ordinary cat now."

Hale's grin grew even wider than before. "On the surface," he said. "Besides, when night returns so will my starlight and my other tail."

I looked at my new best friend, Hale. An ordinary cat by day (if you ignore the fact that he can talk), but come the night he would become a twin-tailed Comet Cat once again. My wish did come true after all!

"Race you to the beach?" I challenged the little black cat with the white-speckled belly.

"You're on!" he answered.

On the count of three, we ran off to find Bob Macy, who would take me and my newfound friend home, together.

***

Tonight, take a moment to stare up at the night sky. If you look up on a clear night, try to find Snake uncoiling in his cosmic nest. In amongst his constellation you will find one star shining brighter than all the rest, which is known by us mortals as 'The Lone Star'. It is a reminder to Snake of all that he has learnt from the little girl called Ebony Night, the Star Pirate; daughter of the land, sea and stars.

This star is Snake's Heart.

The End

Ebony's Legacy:

About the Author

A.C. Winfield (Amy) lived in St.Ives (Porthia) on the west coast of Cornwall, England, for the past 21 years. She now, however, lives in north Devon where most of her influences come from.

At secondary school she was diagnosed with slight dyslexia, which made English and exams a struggle, but determined, she managed to get the GCSEs needed for her college course.

After leaving school, Amy studied an NVQ in photography, and continued her passion for this and art by selling her work at local fairs and events, while sharing her enthusiasm for art with children at schools and clubs.

Since 2006, Amy has had the land of Ia (looking a lot like the outline of Cornwall with influences from north Devon's landscape) floating around and forming inside her head. Characters, creatures and places soon followed the story told to her by Stella.

Along with Stella came Ebony and her legacy.

Amy now uses her artistic and photographic skills to create covers and illustrations for other authors, as well as completing her own children's books.

32380865R00070

Made in the USA
Charleston, SC
17 August 2014